LOVE IS WRETCHED DAHLING

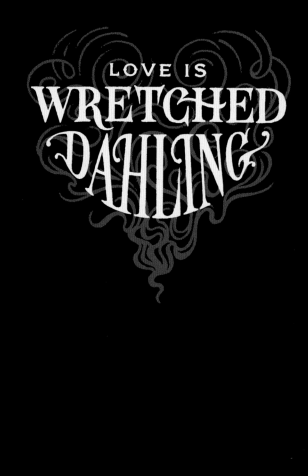

DISNEY
VILLAINS

Happily
Never
After

A Villainous Book of Love and Friendship
for a Very Special Someone

CHRONICLE BOOKS
SAN FRANCISCO

Library of Congress Cataloging-in-Publication Data available.

ISBN 978-1-7972-2344-5

Manufactured in China.

MIX
Paper | Supporting responsible forestry
FSC™ C136333
www.fsc.org

Design by Henna Crowner.

10 9 8 7 6 5 4 3 2 1

Chronicle books and gifts are available at special quantity discounts to corporations, professional associations, literacy programs, and other organizations. For details and discount information, please contact our premiums department at corporatesales@chroniclebooks.com or at 1-800-759-0190.

Chronicle Books LLC
680 Second Street
San Francisco, California 94107
www.chroniclebooks.com

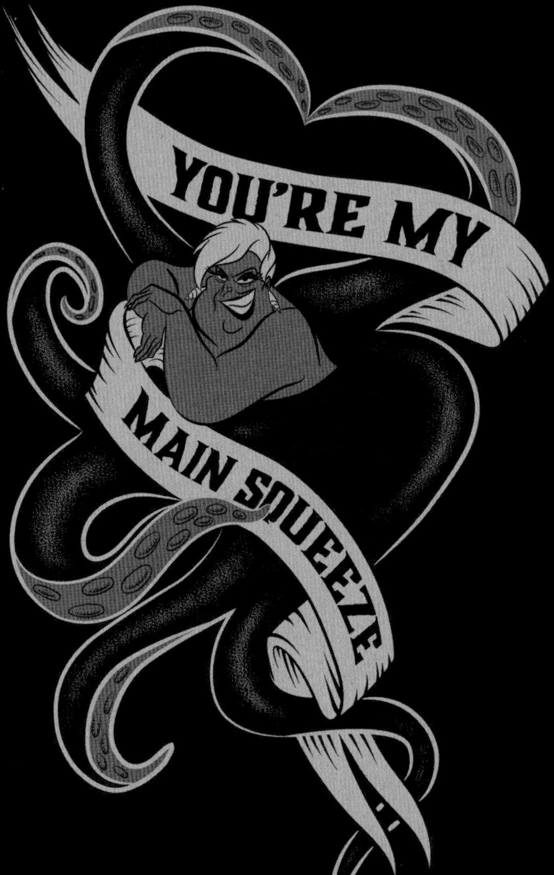
YOU'RE MY
MAIN SQUEEZE

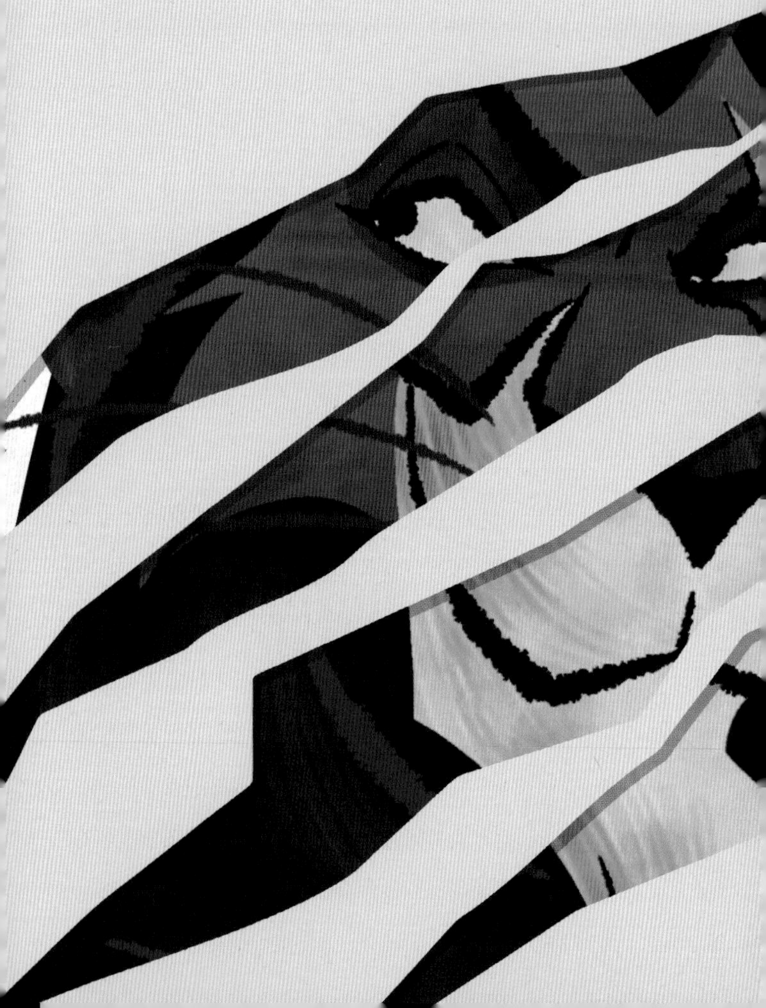

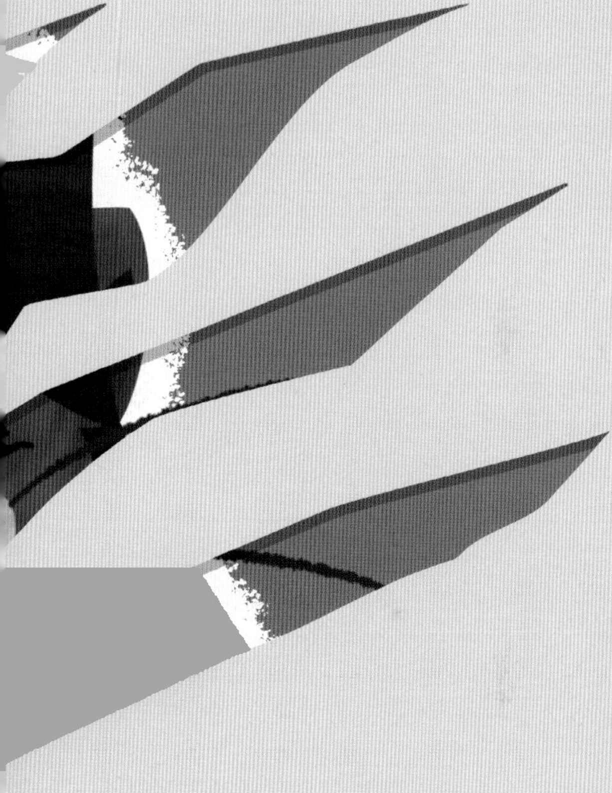

I WON'T BITE

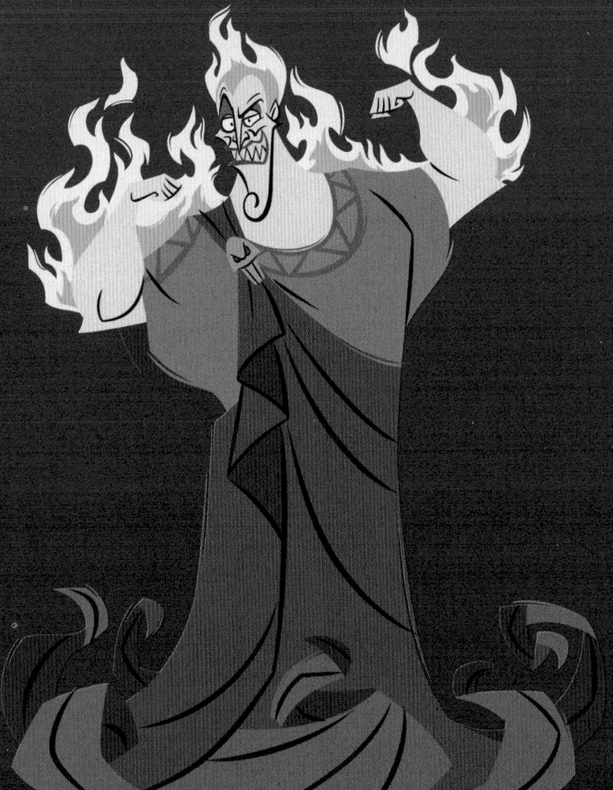

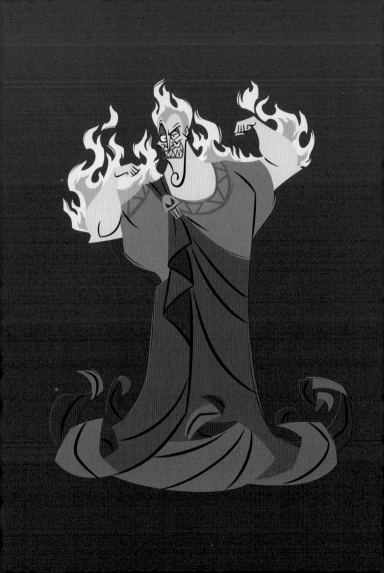

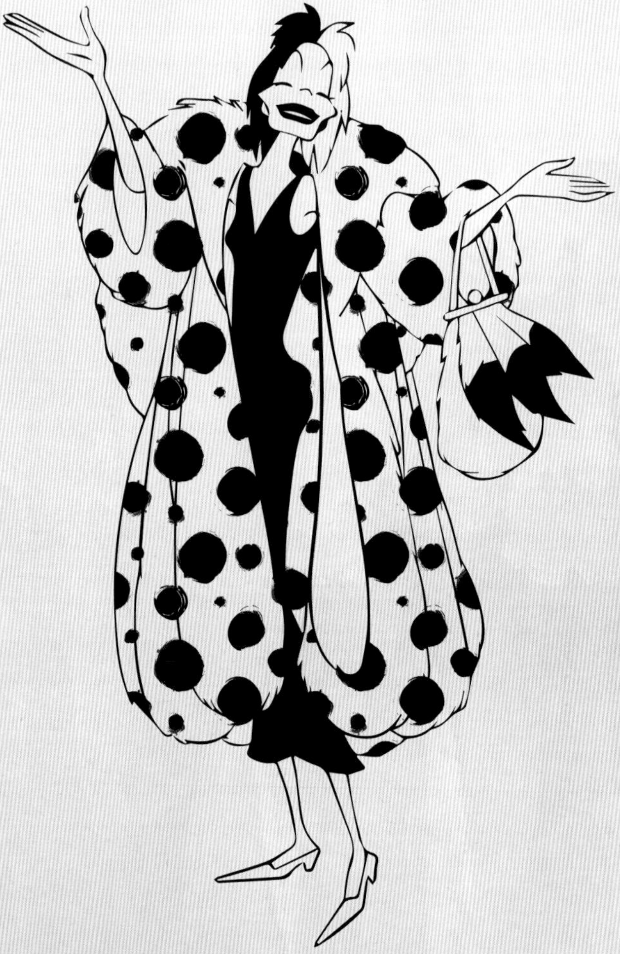

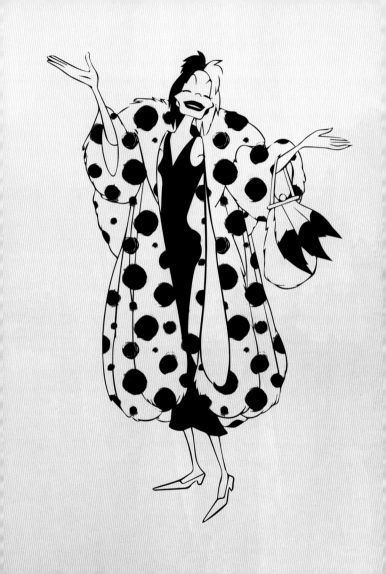

OUR LOVE
NEVER GOES
OUT OF STYLE

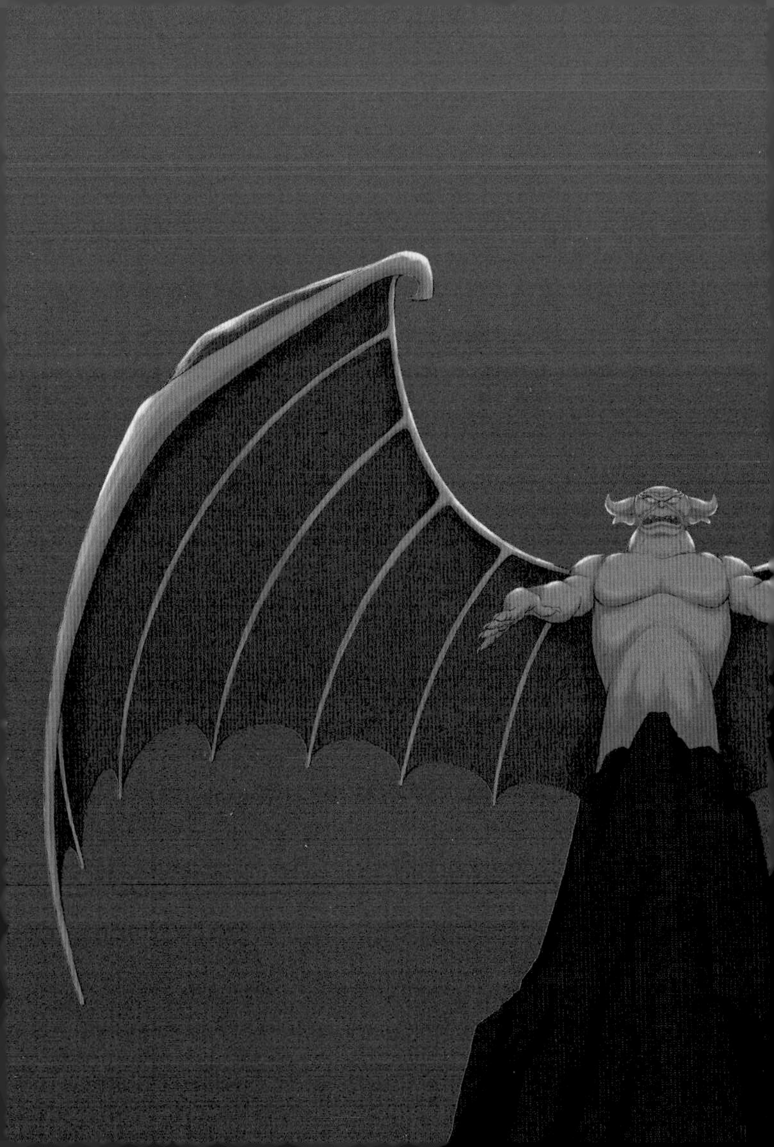

YOU BRING
DARKNESS AND
BURDEN
TO MY
LIFE

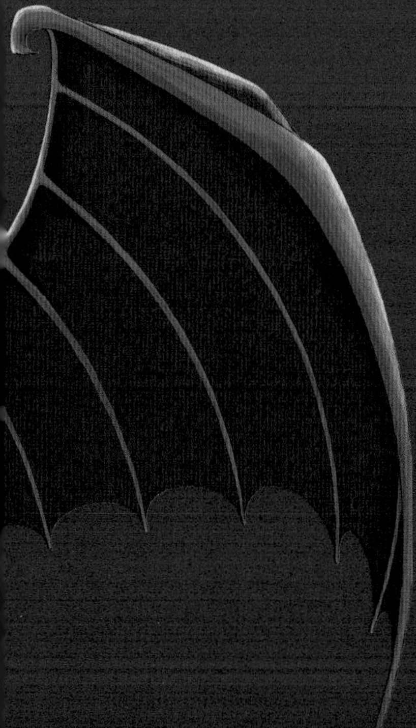

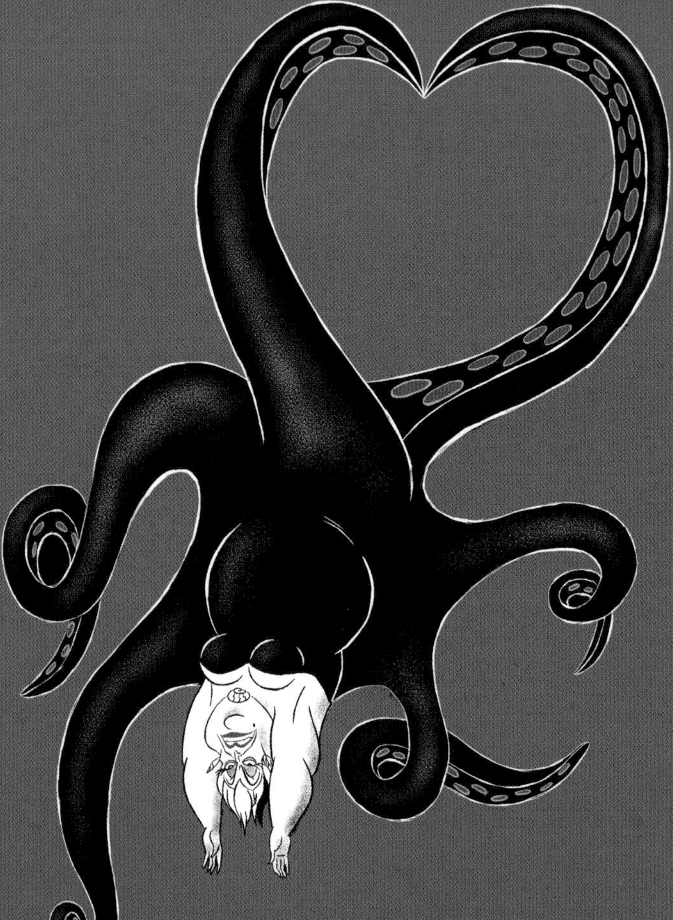

I MISS YOUR VOICE

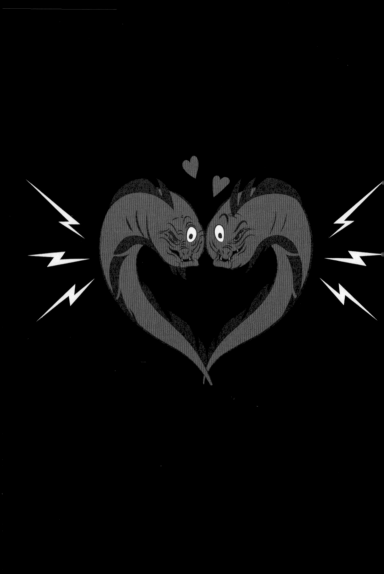

LET'S BE EVIL TOGETHER FOREVER

TRUST SMEE, IT'S NOW OR NEVER LAND

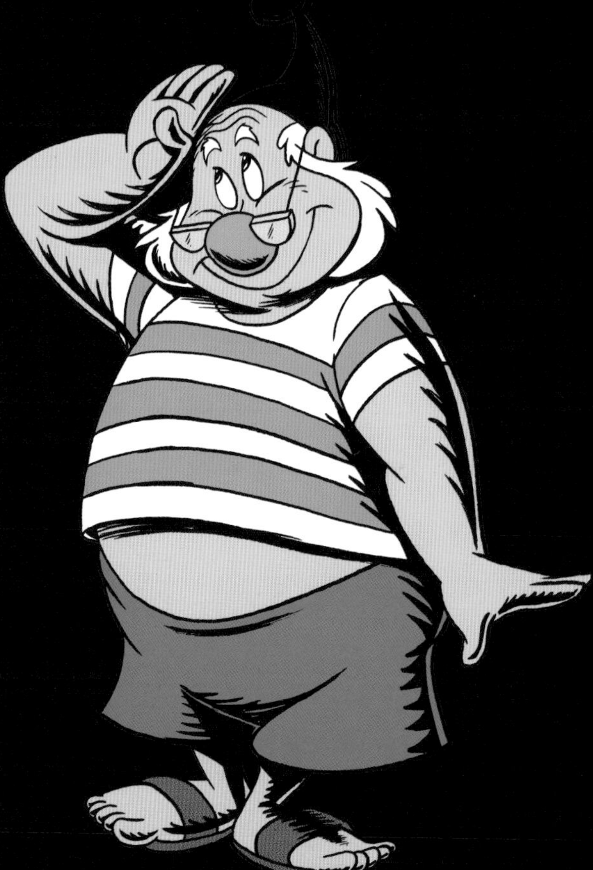

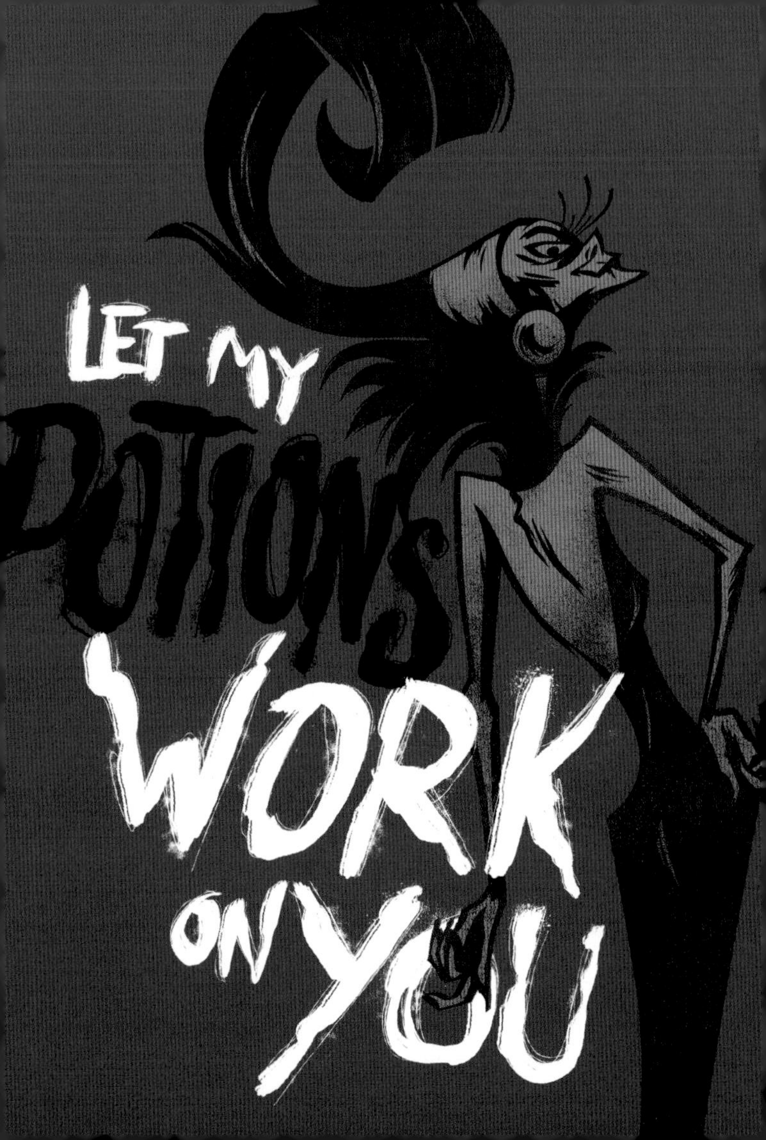
LET MY
POTIONS
WORK
ON YOU

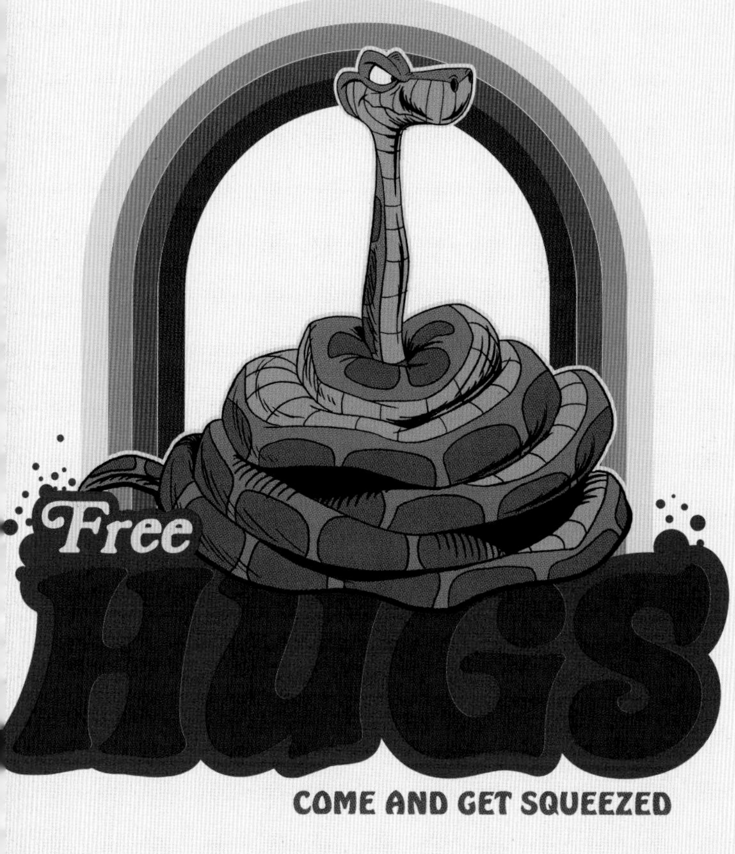
Free
HUGS
COME AND GET SQUEEZED

Cuddle puddle, anyone?

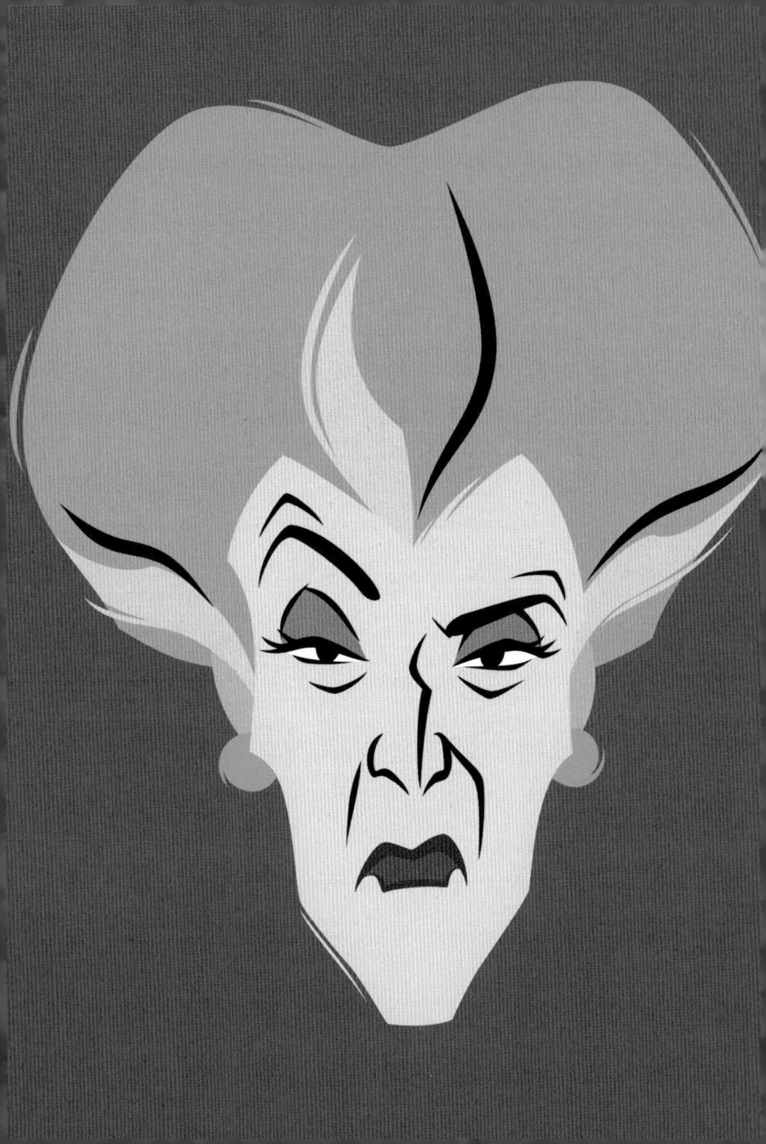

THINKING OF YOU
MAKES ME FEEL ALL
COLD AND WICKED
INSIDE

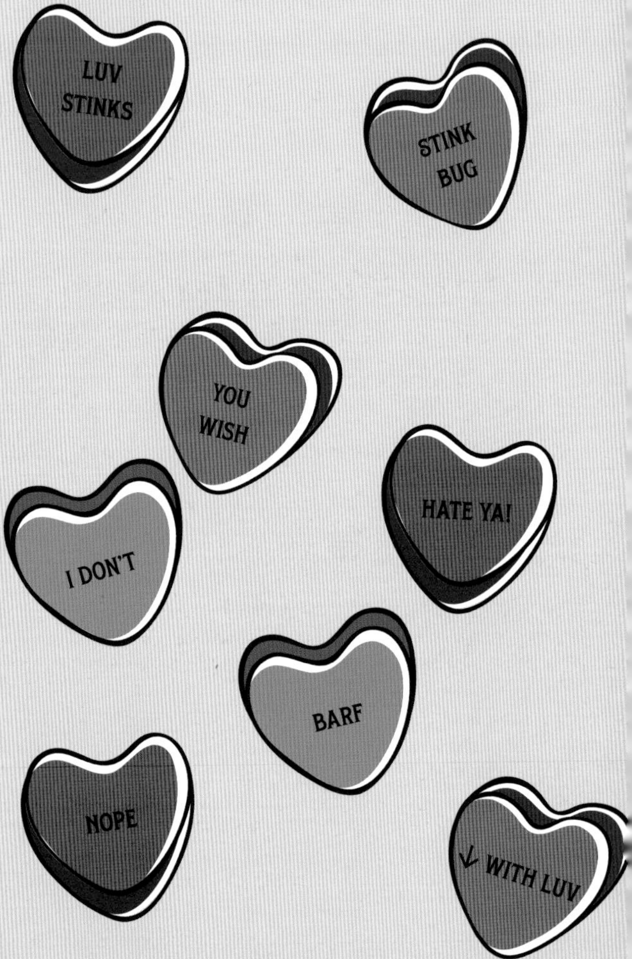
LUV STINKS
STINK BUG
YOU WISH
HATE YA!
I DON'T
BARF
NOPE
WITH LUV

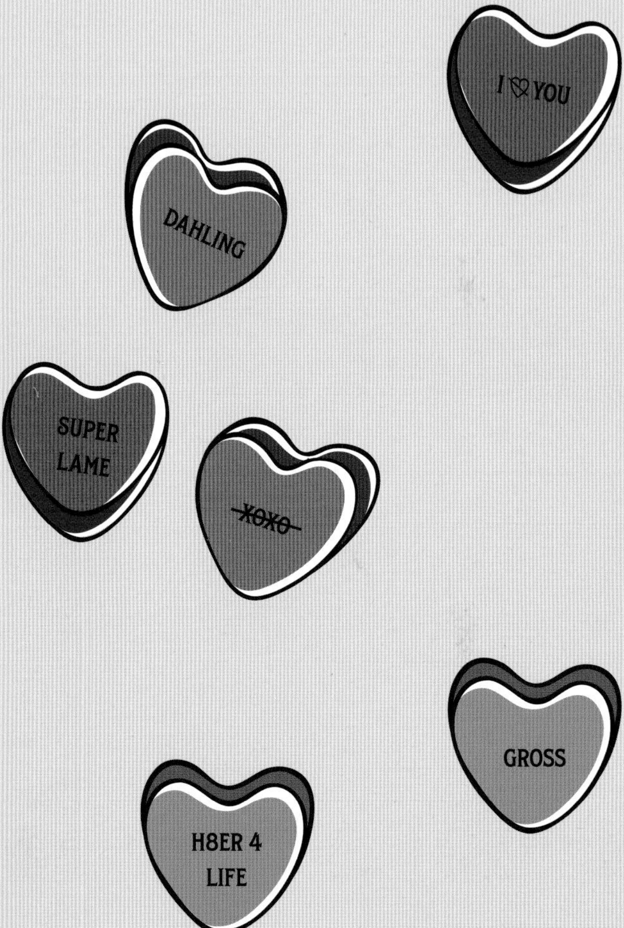
I ♡ YOU
DAHLING
SUPER LAME
~~XOXO~~
GROSS
H8ER 4 LIFE

I'M HOT FOR YOU

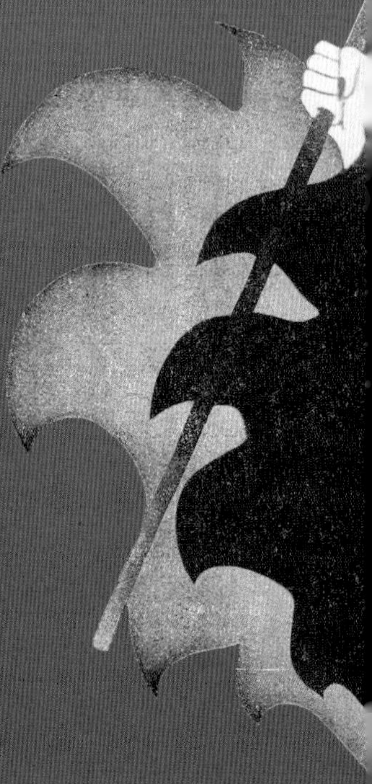

I'VE PUT A SPELL ON YOU

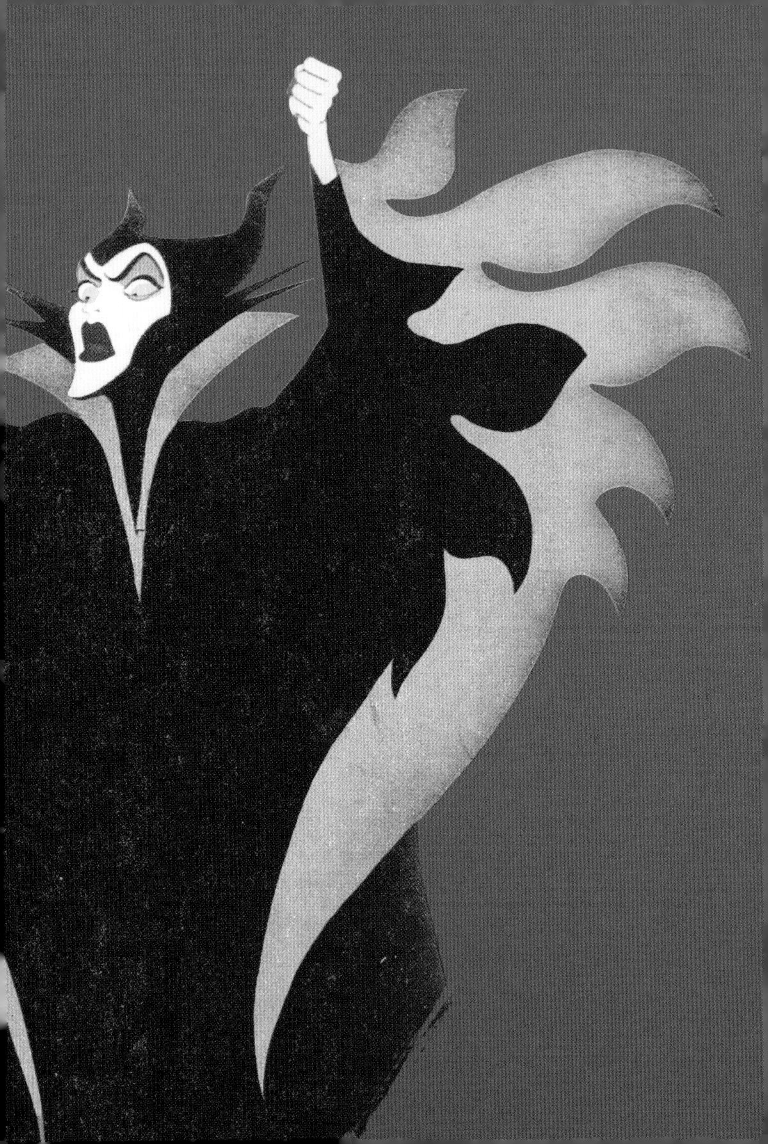

You love me . . .

You love me not . . .

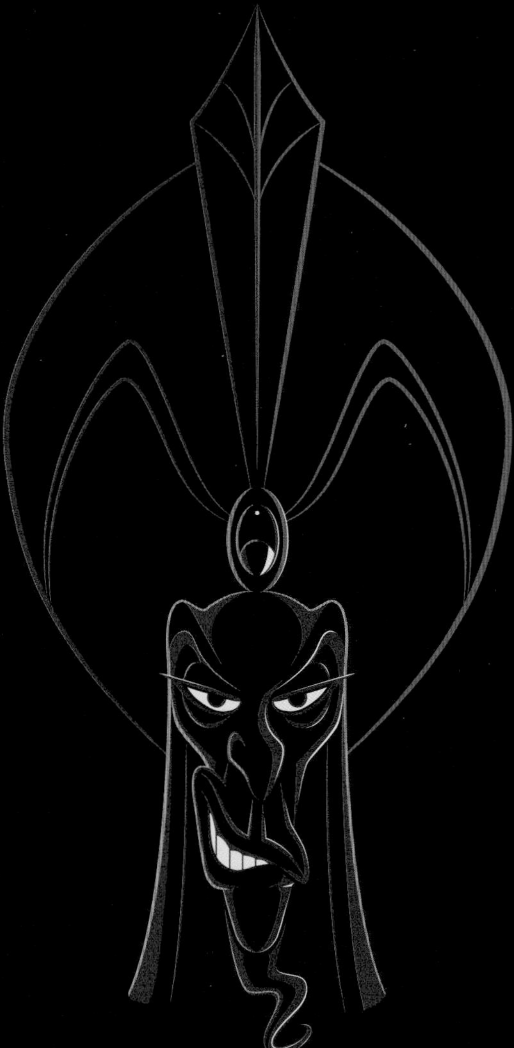

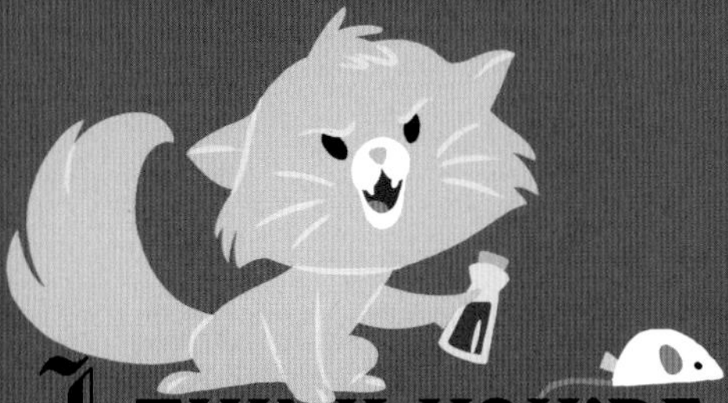

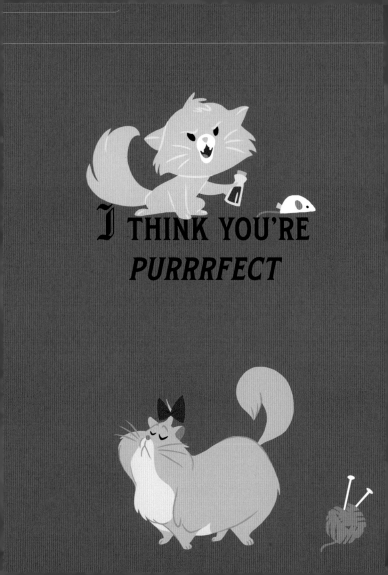

I THINK YOU'RE *PURRRFECT*

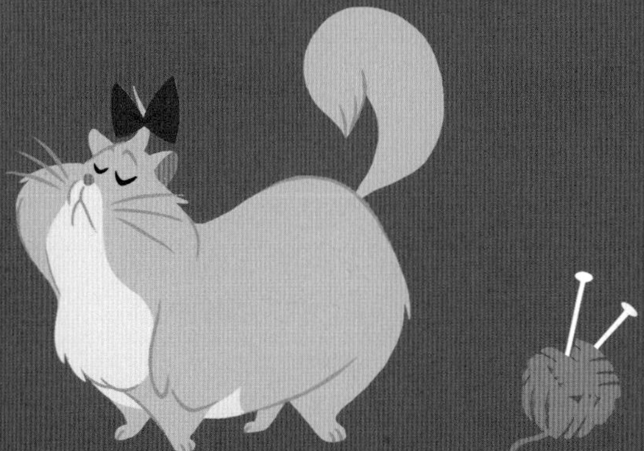

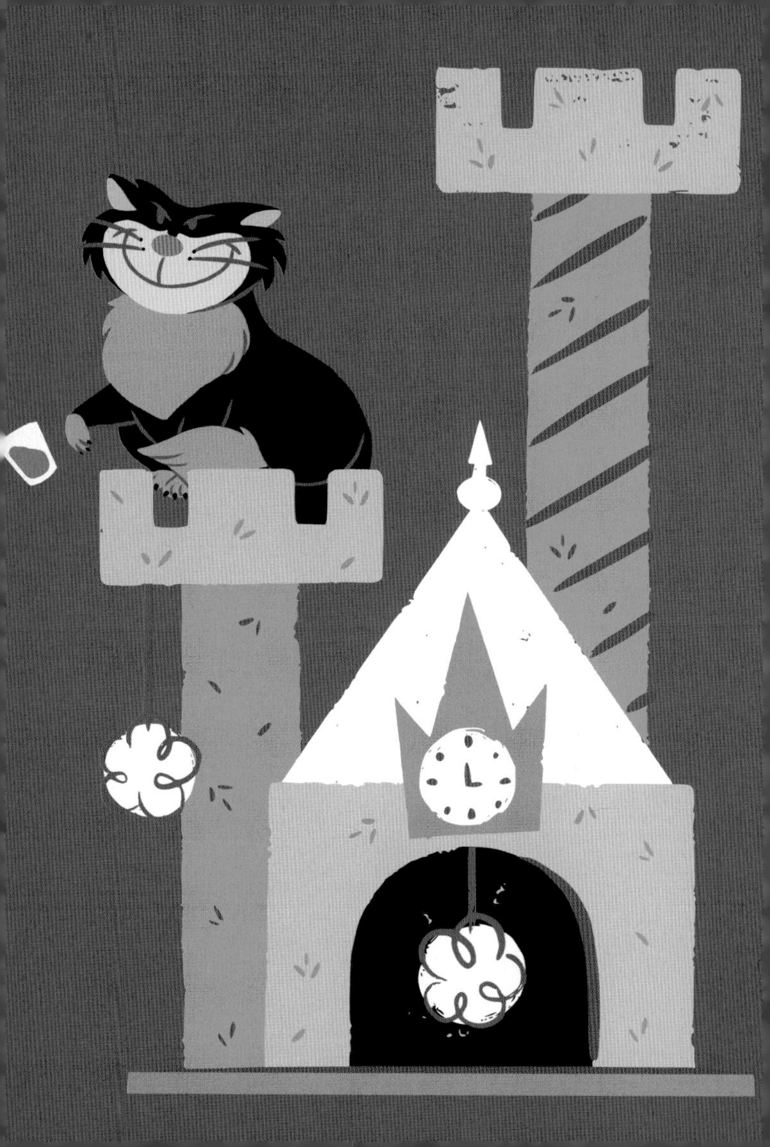

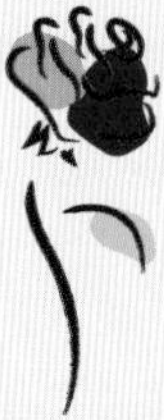

ROSES ARE RED

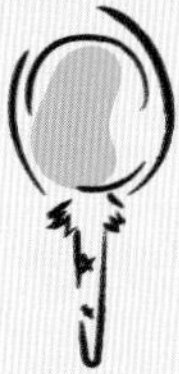

VIOLETS ARE BLUE

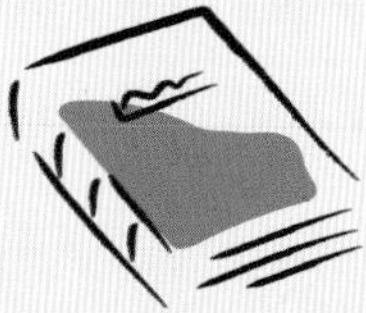

I DESERVE THE BEST

SO I PICK YOU

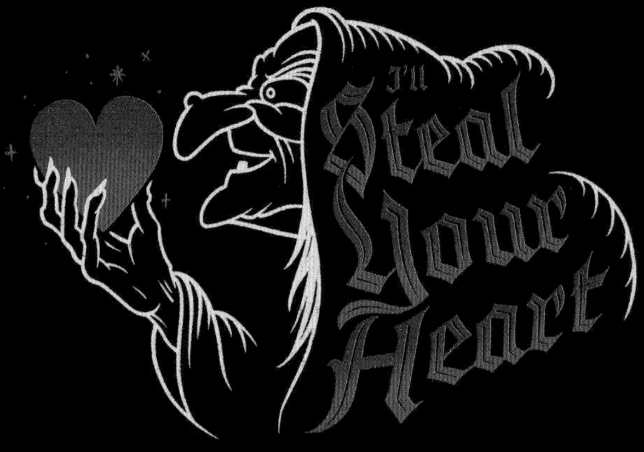
I'll
Steal
Your
Heart

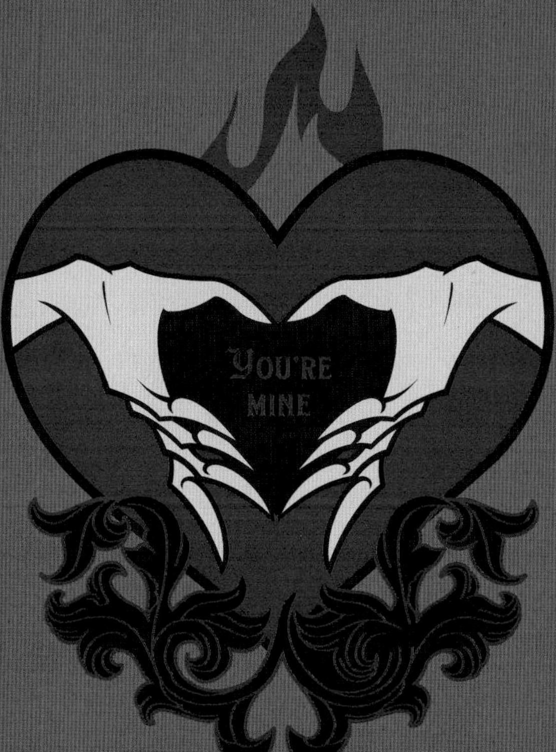
YOU'RE
MINE

CLAIM YOUR ETERNAL REWARD

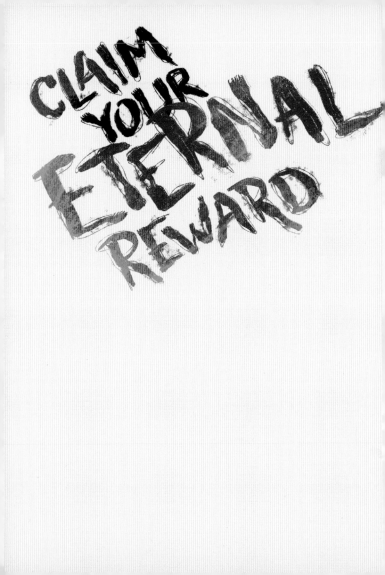

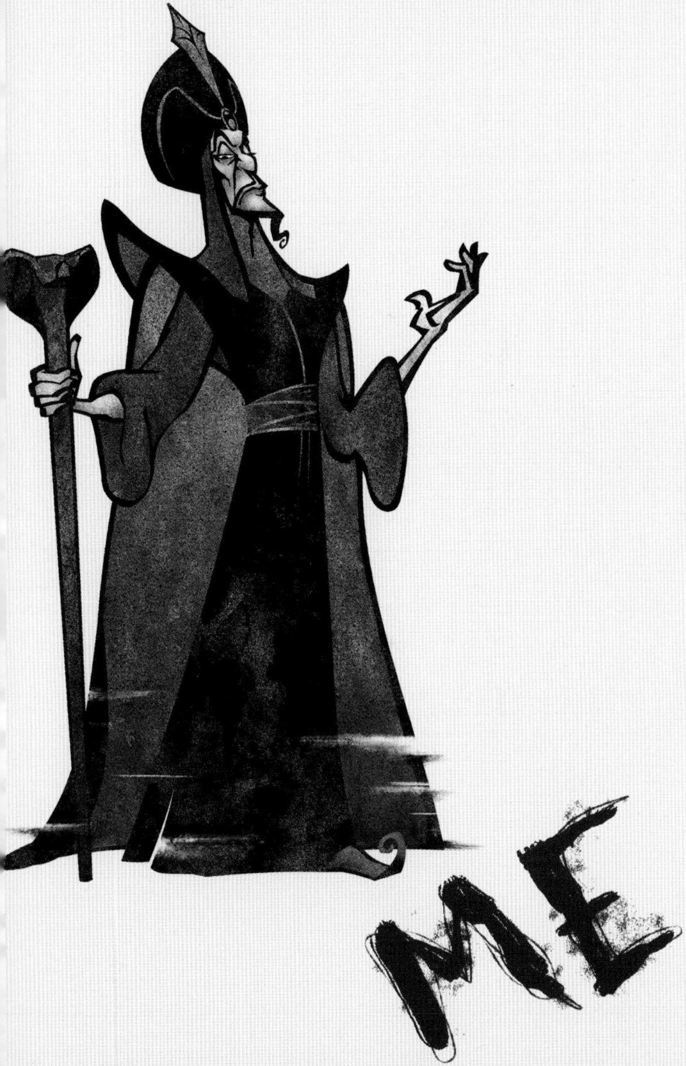
ME

You octopi my heart

I'M HOOKED ON YOU

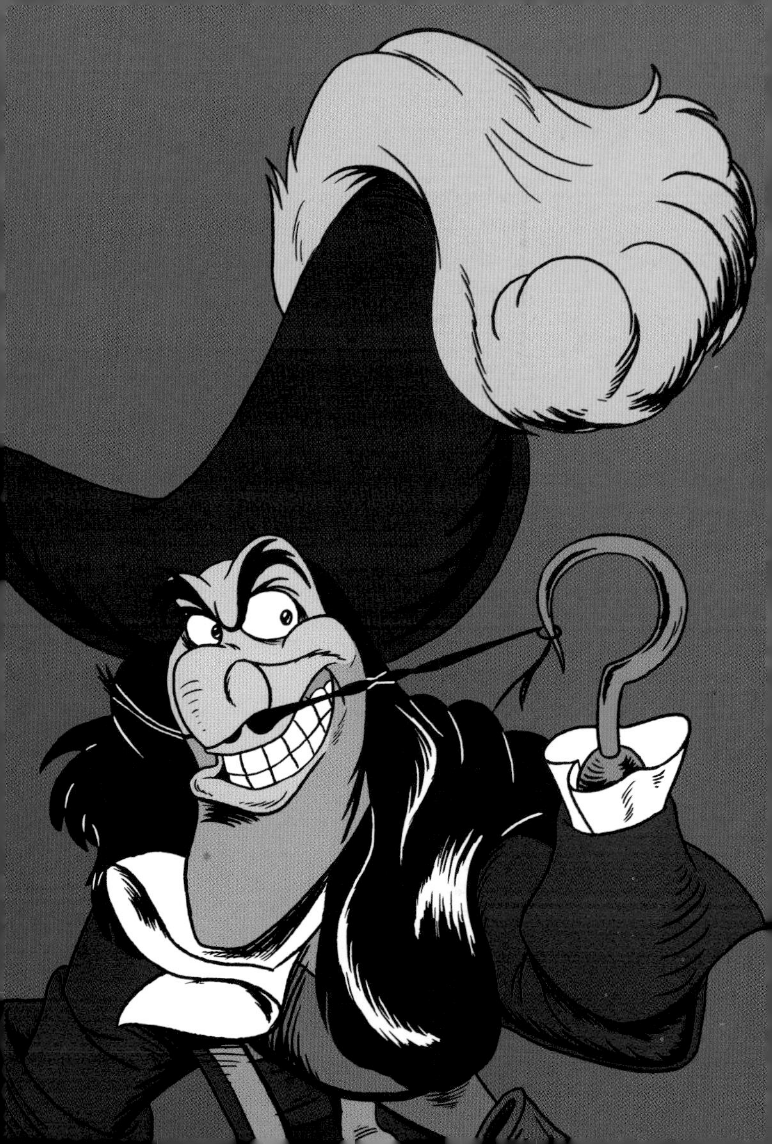

You're one Bad Kitty

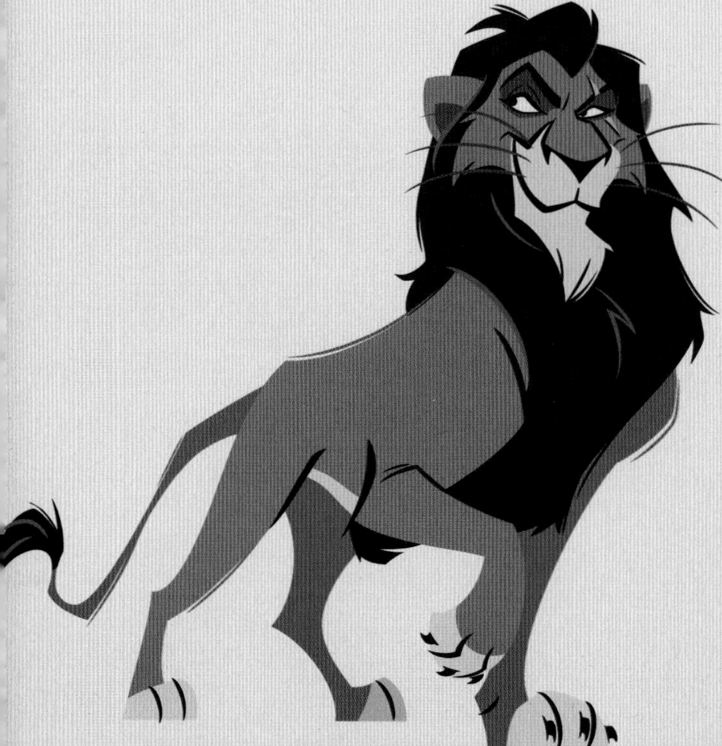

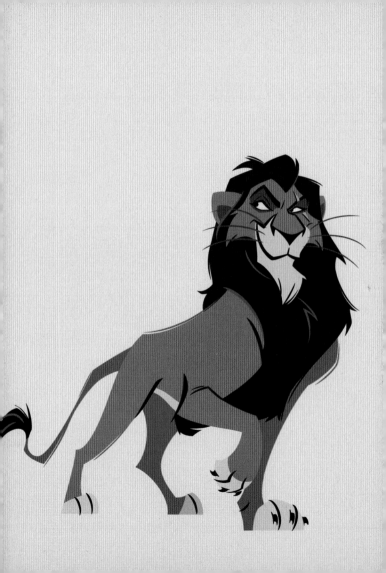

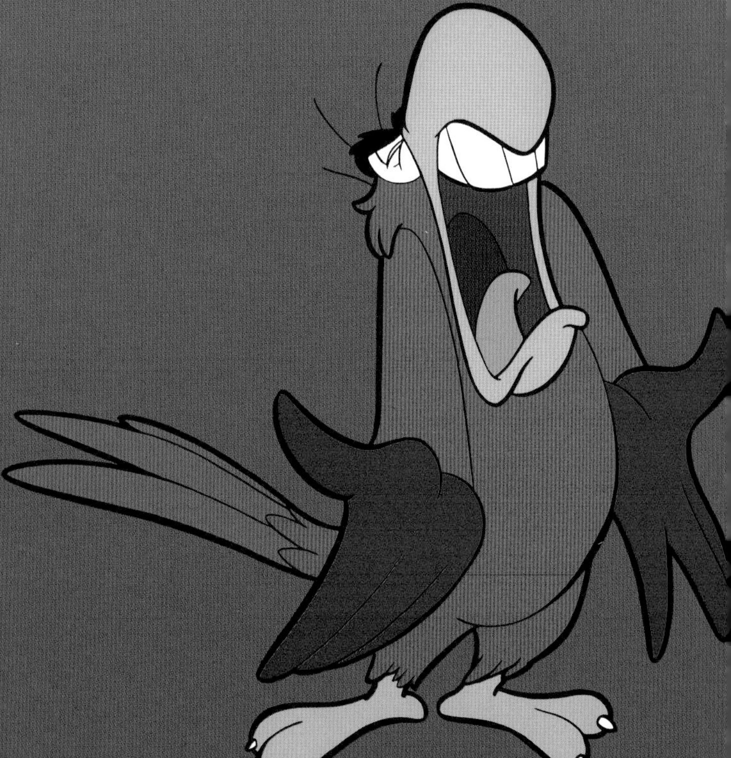

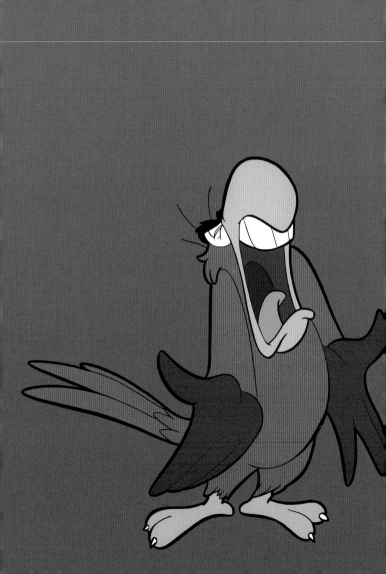

YOUR ROTTENNESS, I'M MOLTING FOR YOU

If I Had a Heart, I'd Give It to You

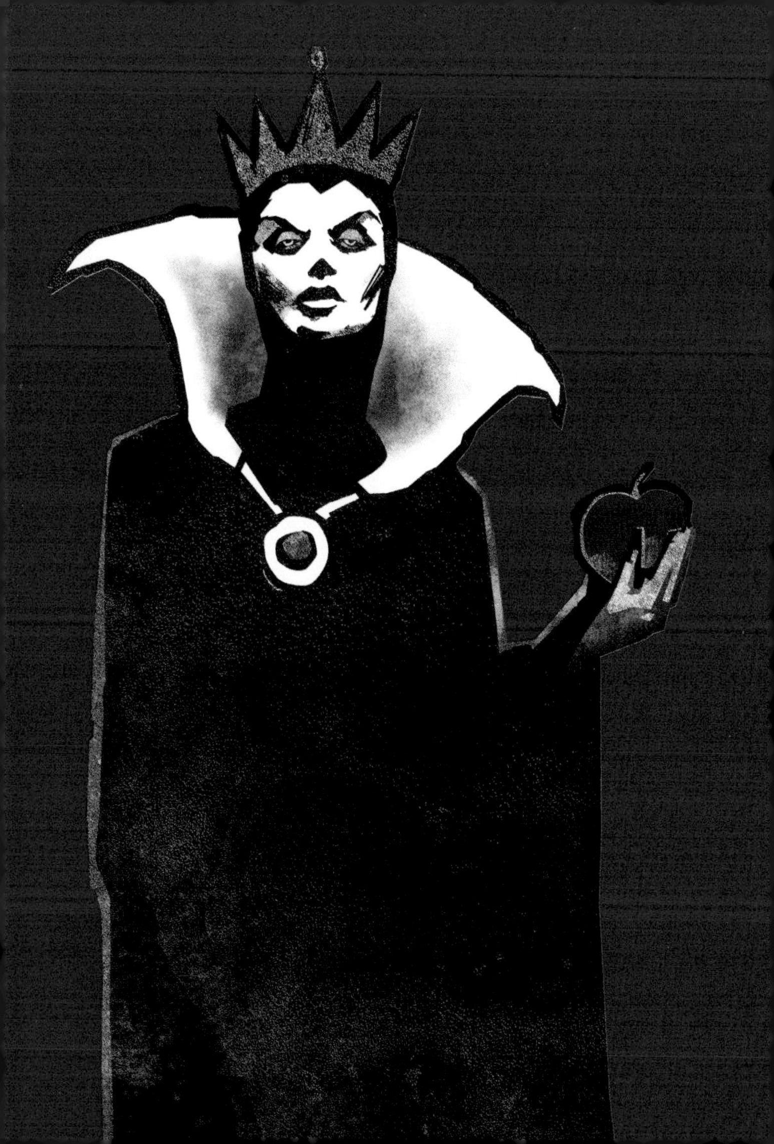

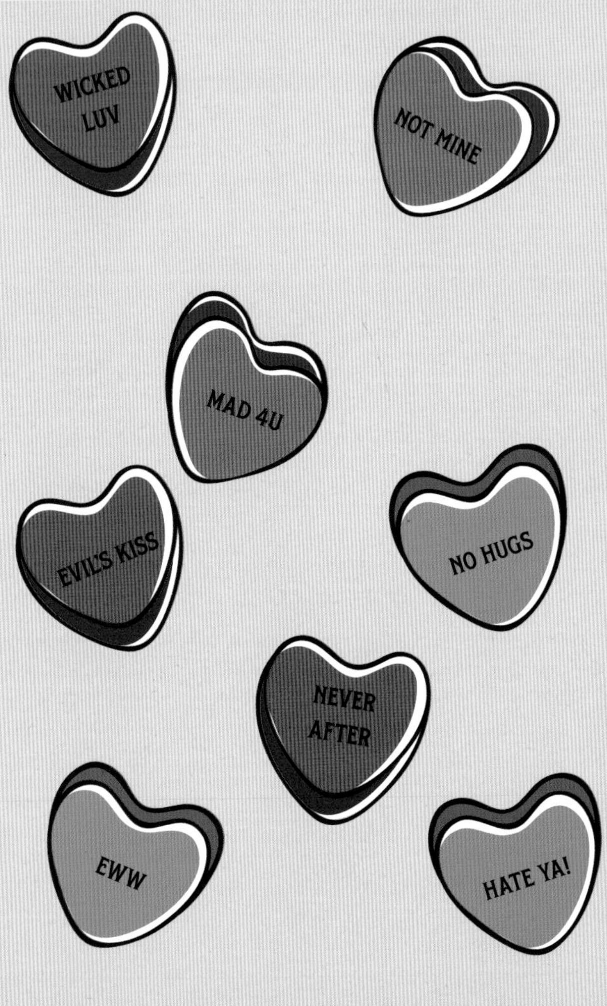
WICKED LUV
NOT MINE
MAD 4U
EVIL'S KISS
NO HUGS
NEVER AFTER
EWW
HATE YA!

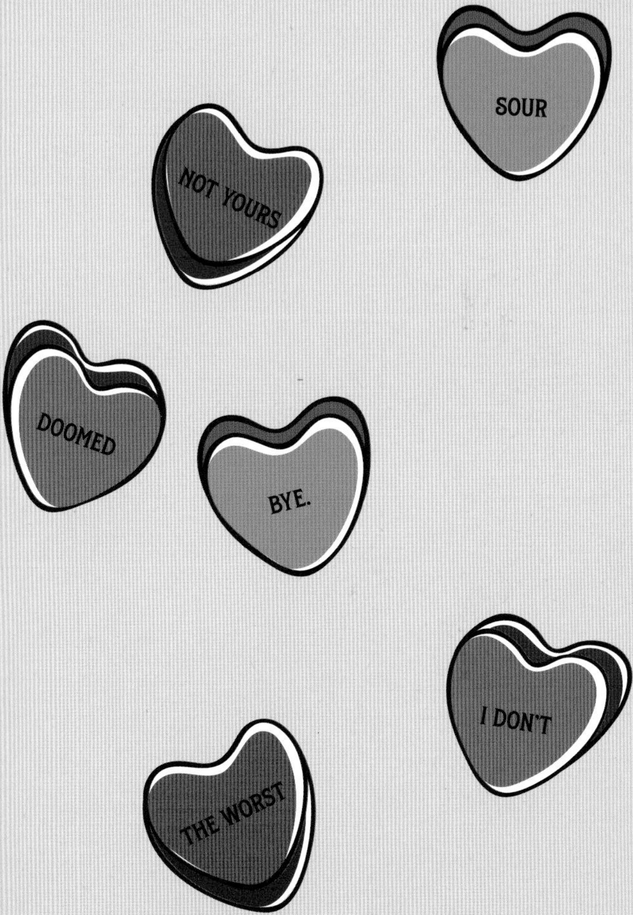
SOUR
NOT YOURS
DOOMED
BYE.
I DON'T
THE WORST

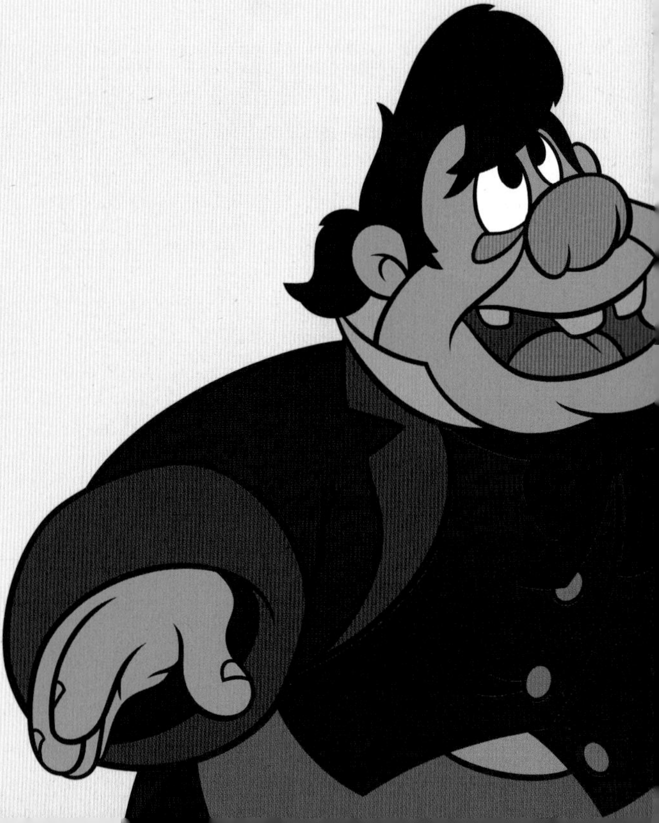

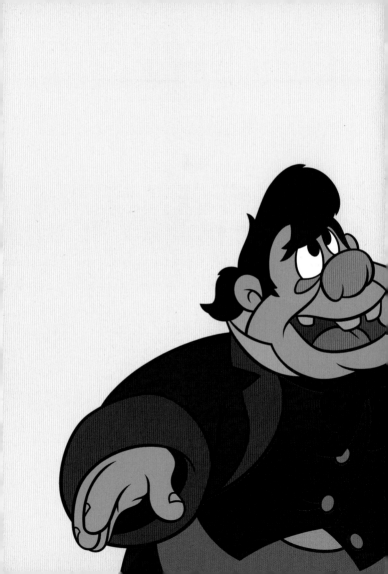

I'M A LE FOU FOR YOU

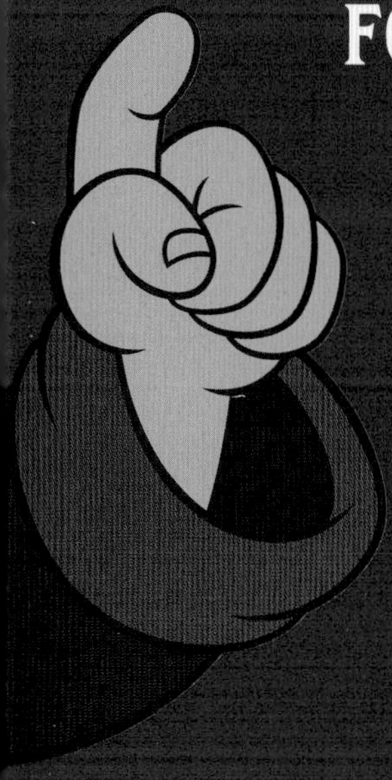

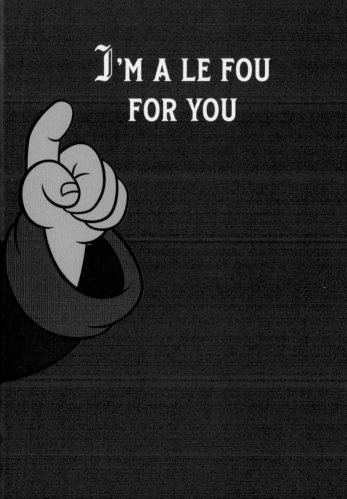

Off with
your heart!

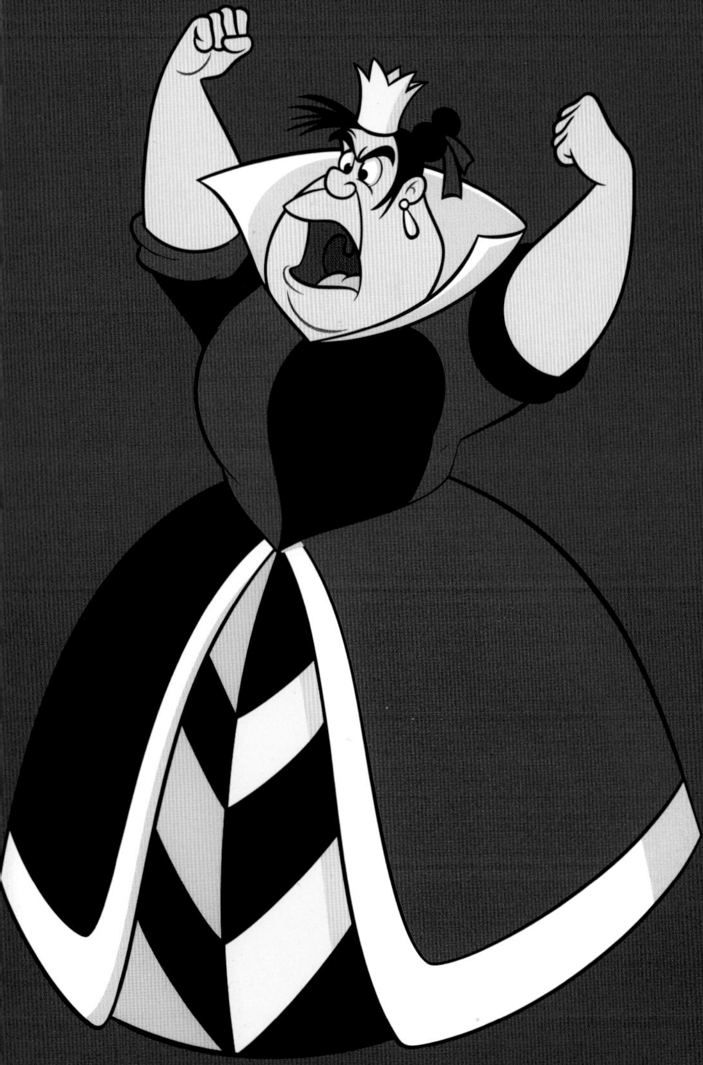

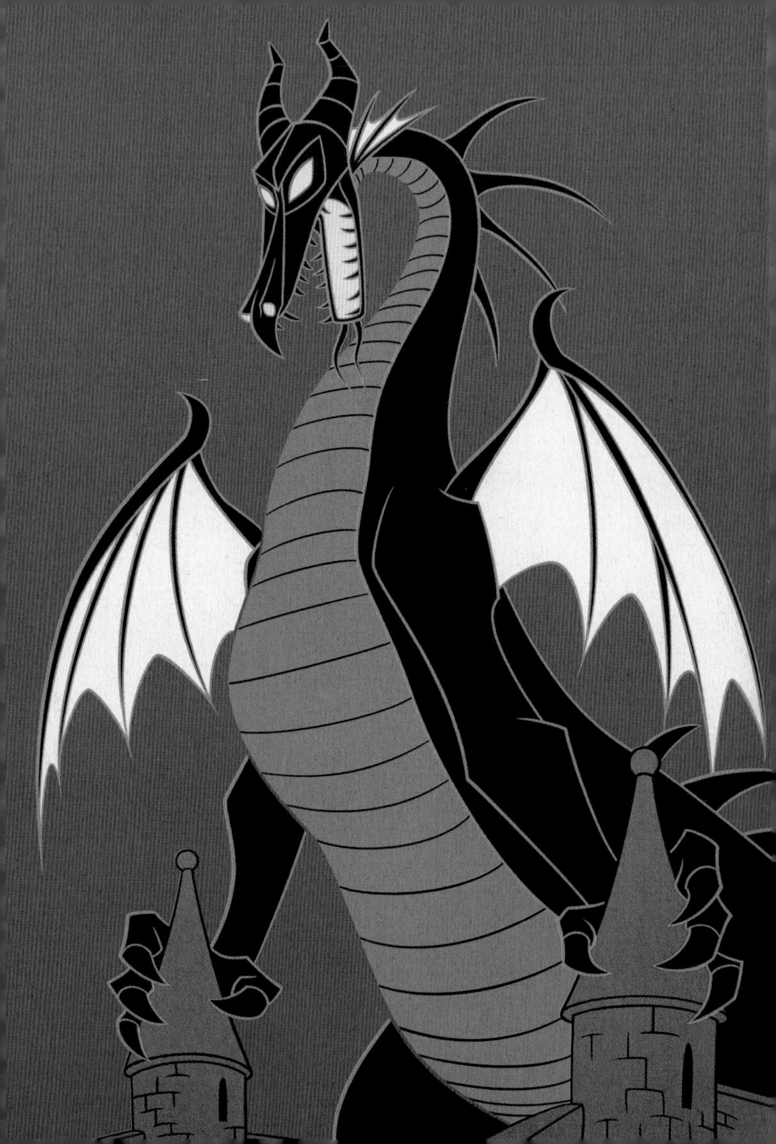

You make my screams come true

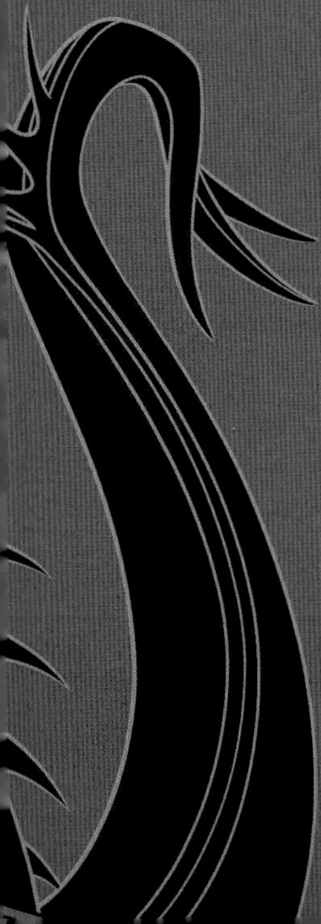

LET'S LIVE HAPPILY NEVER AFTER